SCOOTER
in the Outside

by Anne Bowen

illustrated by Abby Carter

Holiday House / New York

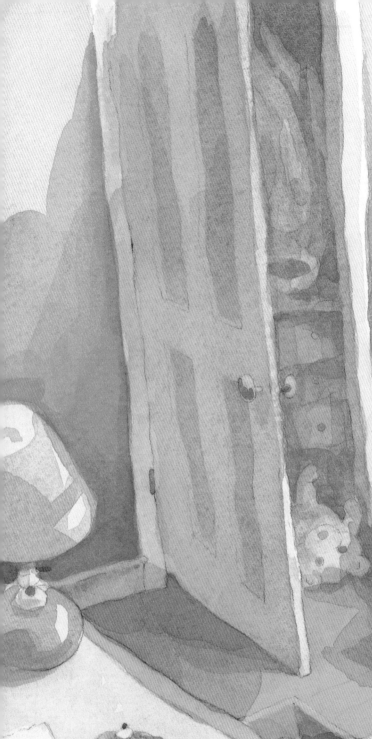

For Liam and Liliana—A. B.
For Duffy, Doug, Samantha, and Carter—A. C.

Text copyright © 2012 by Anne Bowen
Illustrations copyright © 2012 by Abby Carter
All Rights Reserved
HOLIDAY HOUSE is registered in the U.S. Patent and Trademark Office.
Printed and Bound in November 2011 at Tien Wah Press, Johor Bahru,
Johor, Malaysia.
The text typeface is Hank BT.
The illustrations were created with watercolors and black colored pencil.
www.holidayhouse.com
First Edition
1 3 5 7 9 10 8 6 4 2

Library of Congress Cataloging-in-Publication Data
Bowen, Anne, 1952-
Scooter in the outside / by Anne Bowen ; illustrated by Abby Carter. — 1st ed.
ISBN 978-0-8234-2326-2 (hardcover)
[1. Dogs—Fiction. 2. Human-animal relationships—Fiction.] I. Carter, Abby, ill. II. Title.
PZ7.B671945Sco 2012
[E]—dc22
2010030764

Ba-DUMP, ba-DUMP, ba-DUMP! Scooter
ran up the stairs, down the hall, and around
the corner. He wagged his tail. THWAPPA-
THWAPPA-THUMP!

"Ready to go outside?" Lucy asked.

Scooter said, "Yes! Yes-yes!" But what
came out was this: "WOOF! WOOF-WOOF!"

Lucy opened the door, and there it was . . .
THE OUTSIDE! Scooter sniff-sniffed the air.
He wagged his tail. *THWAPPA-THWAPPA-THUMP!*
He tugged at his leash.

The two friends headed down the sidewalk.
Lucy skipped and Scooter ran, but not too fast.

They passed Miss Winthrop's house. Her teeny dogs, Bitty and Bitsy, raced up and down the fence. "You can't get us!" they said, but what came out was this: "YAPPA-YAPPA-YAP!"

Scooter sniff-sniffed here. There.
Everywhere.
Lucy sang: "Scooteree-Scooteroo,
Forever friends, I love yooooou."

Soon they came to THE CORNER.
"This is where we turn around," Lucy said.
"NO!" Scooter barked back. But what came
out was this: "ARF!"

Lucy tugged. Scooter pulled.
"HOME!" Lucy said.
"ARF!" Scooter barked.
"*Scooter!*" Lucy said firmly.

Scooter turned around. But he didn't want to.

At home Lucy gave Scooter two doggy snacks and filled his blue bowl with water.

When it was time for bed, she
kissed the top of his furry head.
   "Sweet dreams for the sweetest
dog," she whispered.
   Scooter kissed her back. *SLOPPITY-*
SLURP!

And then he fell fast asleep. Scooter dreamed
he was in THE OUTSIDE. He dreamed he was
running here. There. Everywhere.

One morning Lucy ran past Scooter.
"I'm late for school!" she said.

Scooter sighed, "Haaaaa-rumph,"
and paced the floor.

That's when he saw the door. It was open!
To THE OUTSIDE!

One paw, then another, and another and another . . .

and then Scooter was in THE OUTSIDE.
He wagged his tail. THWAPPA-THWAPPA-
THWAPPA!

Scooter raced down the sidewalk past Bitty and Bitsy.
"YAP-YAPPA-YAP!"

Faster and faster Scooter ran.

Suddenly he slid to a stop. Scooter had reached
THE CORNER.

"Huh-huh-huh!"
he panted.

He looked behind him
and then in front of him.

"Could I? Should I?" he
thought.
He paced back and forth,
back and forth. "Huh-huh-huh."

And then he did it! Scooter leaped across the street to THE OTHER SIDE.

Scooter bounded down the sidewalk.
"Look at me! Look at me!" he barked to the
world. But what came out was this: "WOOFA-
WOOFA-WOOFA!"

Scooter ran through a sprinkler.

He lay down in the grass and rolled around and around. Stretch. Scratch. Shake. Oh! THE OUTSIDE felt good.

WEEEEE-OOOOOO-WEEEEE-OOOOO!
Scooter jumped up, up in the air. His heart
pounded. A giant something roared past him
down the street.

"AAAAAAA-ROOOOOOO," Scooter howled.

BEEP-BEEP-BEEP!
Another giant something
rumbled to a stop at the curb.
This time Scooter ran and hid.
He watched the giant something open
its wide mouth. *BEEP-BEEP-BEEP!*

Scooter whimpered. He lay down beneath
a tree. THE OTHER SIDE was mean and
loud and scary.

"Scooter?"

Scooter raised his big head. He couldn't believe his floppy ears.

"What are *you* doing *here*?" Lucy said.

Scooter took a big breath. "The doorwasopento THEOUTSIDE Iranandranpast thedogs,pastTHE CORNER,downthe street.Agiantsome thingwentWOOOOO EEEEEEandanother giantsomething . . ." But what came out was this: "*WOOF-WOOF-ARF-WOOF-WOOF-ARF-WOOF-AAAA-ROOOO!*"

Lucy wrapped her arms around Scooter's neck and hugged him. "Shhh . . . ," she said softly. "It's okay. You're with me now."

Scooter walked beside Lucy all the way
home—past the sprinkler, past Bitsy and Bitty.
"Next time," Lucy said, "let's cross to THE
OTHER SIDE together. How does that sound?"
"WOOF!" Scooter answered.

When they got home, Scooter was too tired for doggy snacks, but not for big gulps of water from his blue bowl.

At bedtime Scooter could barely keep his eyes open. He barely heard "Sweet dreams for the sweetest dog." But he could feel Lucy gently stroking his furry head.

"Woof-woof," Scooter said before drifting off to sleep. And Lucy knew exactly what that meant. "I love you too," she whispered.